Tanya and the Red Shoes

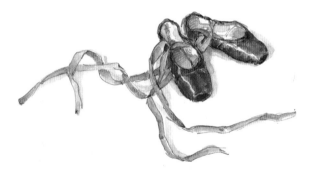

Tanya

and the

Red Shoes

PATRICIA LEE GAUCH

illustrated by SATOMI ICHIKAWA

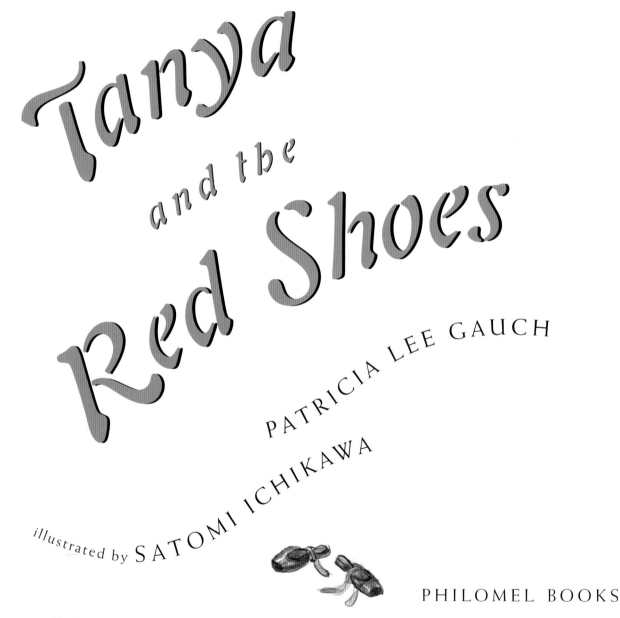

PHILOMEL BOOKS

I am Tanya. I have danced in recitals in soft pink ballet slippers. I have danced barefoot all alone in front of my mother's mirror, and in sneakers with my friends—girls and boys—to music we love.

But I have never danced on toe shoes! Oh, I want to! My sister Elise does, why not me? "You aren't ready to go *sur pointes*," my teacher always says.

Sur pointes means dancing on my toes. "One day, perhaps," she says.
One day seems a long, long way off.

And then I see the ballet *The Red Shoes*
on television. The ballerina whirls and whirls on
the tips of her toes—her shoes are a most wonderful red.

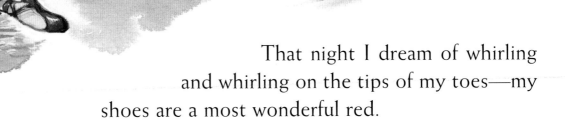

That night I dream of whirling
and whirling on the tips of my toes—my
shoes are a most wonderful red.

But when I wake up, there are my old ballet slippers at the end of my bed. They are pink and worn, and have no ribbons. "You are too young for toe," Elise says to me when I tell her about my dream. "One day, perhaps."

One day is just too far away!

So after each class I begin to watch Elise's class *sur pointes.*
At home I dance on tiptoe all around the dining room table, pretending
I am dancing in my own "red shoes."

Then one spring day Ms. Foley gathers everyone around her and says,
"You are going to begin to dance on toe. Please get your shoes this week."

My heart is bursting! Finally.

My mother goes with me to pick out my shoes.
On the way to the next class I hold them to me as if they are flowers.

Then Ms. Foley lets us rise to our toes in dance class.

Oh, my! I am so tall! Like a queen! And when the music plays, I think that I can fly!

But then it is over
before I can.
    "Only five minutes today," Ms.
Foley says. And we all come down
and are elephants walking across the floor.
Clunk, clunk, clunk.

Not only do my toes pinch, I have a blister—two!
This is not at all like my red shoes dream.

That night I soak my toes in warm water, and that night I do not dream at all. The next class is the same, and the next. And while I still hang my shoes at the end of my bed, and sometimes cradle them like flowers, I begin to wonder what is so magic about toe shoes after all.

One day I throw them across the room!

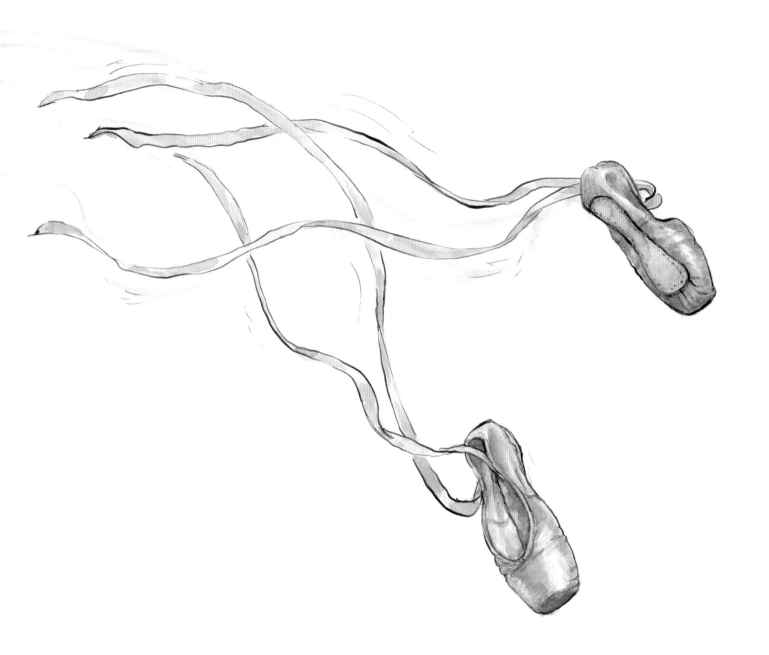

But Elise sees me.
She holds my toe
shoes for a few min-
utes. Then she holds
her hand out to me.
"Let's dance," she says.

And we dance together to music with violins.

And then she says, "Watch me." She rises on toe, walking like a queen.
Then to violins, she turns and turns again.

And then she pulls back, and flies in a leap that I have never seen her do. Ah, I think, that is the magic. She flies, my sister.

When the music ends, she says, "It just takes time."

And so the days
pass, and the weeks pass, and
my blisters grow hard, and I dance
longer and longer *sur pointes*.
Until the day comes when I forget the blisters,
and the squeezed toes, and I am not an elephant.

And the night comes when I have another dream. It is the dancer with the red shoes, but the dancer is me.

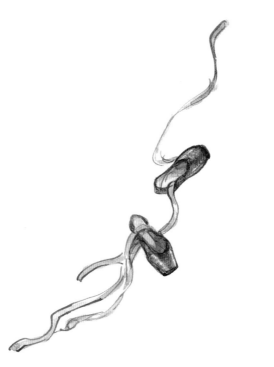

Text copyright © 2002 by Patricia Lee Gauch.
Illustrations copyright © 2002 by Satomi Ichikawa. All rights reserved.
This book, or parts thereof, may not be reproduced in any form without
permission in writing from the publisher,
PHILOMEL BOOKS
a division of Penguin Putnam Books for Young Readers,
345 Hudson Street, New York, NY 10014.
Philomel Books, Reg. U.S. Pat. & Tm. Off. Published simultaneously in Canada.
Printed in Hong Kong by South China Printing Co. (1988) Ltd.
Book design by Semadar Megged.
The text is set in 17-point Weiss.

Library of Congress Cataloging-in-Publication Data
Gauch, Patricia Lee. Tanya and the red shoes / Patricia Lee Gauch ; illustrated by Satomi Ichikawa.
p. cm.   Summary: Tanya wants to dance in toe shoes the way her sister does.
[1. Ballet dancing—Fiction. 2. Dancers—Fiction. 3. Sisters—Fiction.] I. Ichikawa, Satomi, ill. II. Title.
PZ7.G2315 Taq 2002   [E]—dc21   2001033916   ISBN 0-399-23314-8
1 3 5 7 9 10 8 6 4 2
First Impression

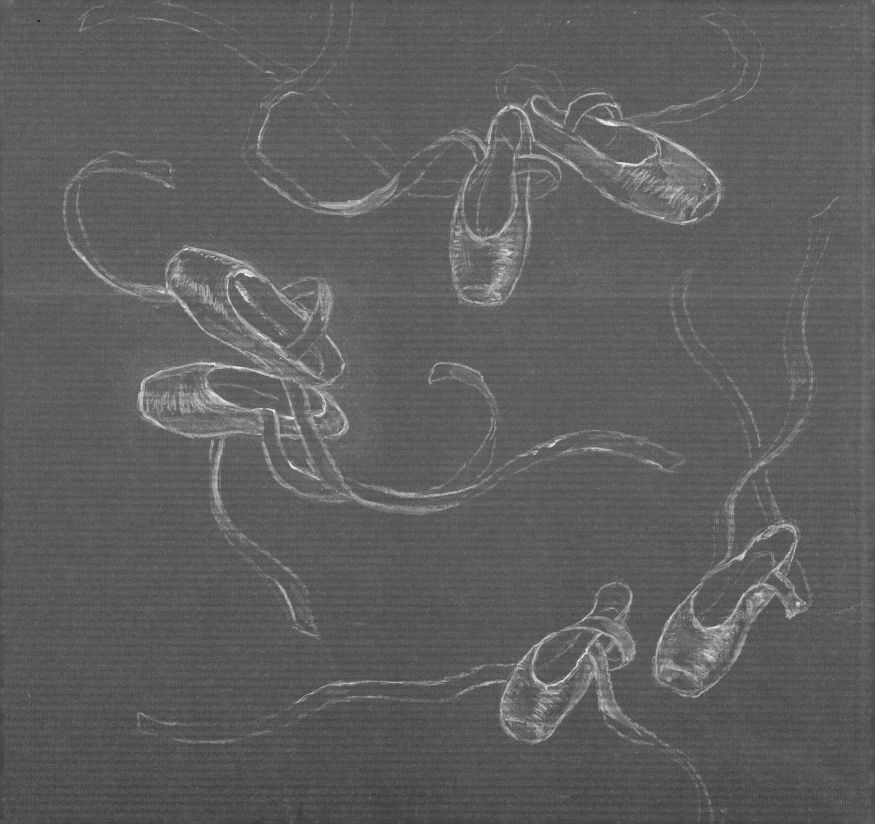